GREEK BEASTS AND HEROES

The One-Eyed Giant

You can read the stories in the **Greek Beasts and Heroes** series in any order.

If you'd like to read more about some of the characters in this book, turn to pages 77–79 to find out which other books to try.

Atticus's journey continues on from *The Hero's Spear.*

His quest ends in *The Sailor Snatchers.*

Also in the series:

1. *The Beasts in the Jar*
2. *The Magic Head*
3. *The Monster in the Maze*
4. *The Dolphin's Message*
5. *The Silver Chariot*
6. *The Fire Breather*
7. *The Flying Horse*
8. *The Harp of Death*
9. *The Dragon's Teeth*
10. *The Hero's Spear*
11. *The One-Eyed Giant*
12. *The Sailor Snatchers*

GREEK BEASTS AND HEROES

The One-Eyed Giant

LUCY COATS

Illustrated by Anthony Lewis

Orion
Children's Books

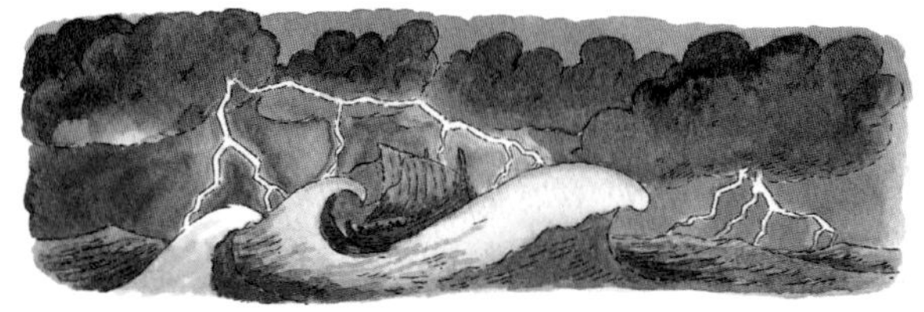

Text and illustrations first appeared in
Atticus the Storyteller's 100 Greek Myths
First published in Great Britain in 2002
by Orion Children's Books
This edition published in Great Britain in 2010
by Orion Children's Books
a division of the Orion Publishing Group Ltd
Orion House
5 Upper St Martin's Lane
London WC2H 9EA
An Hachette UK company

1 3 5 7 9 8 6 4 2

The Orion Publishing Group's policy is to use papers that are natural, renewable and recyclable products and made from wood grown in sustainable forests. The logging and manufacturing processes are expected to conform to the environmental regulations of the country of origin.

A catalogue record for this book is available from the British Library

ISBN 978 1 4440 0075 7

Printed in China

www.orionbooks.co.uk
www.lucycoats.com

For my darling Archie,
who loves stories too.

L. C.

For John

A. L.

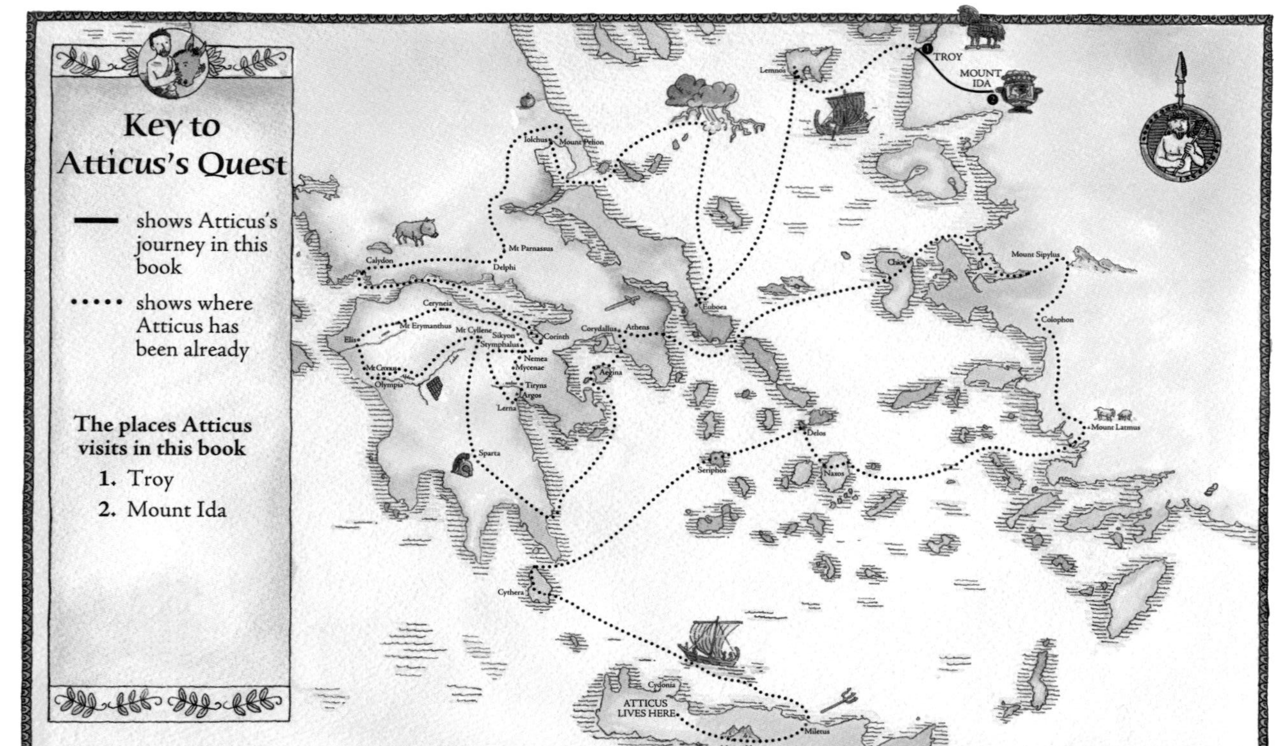

Key to Atticus's Quest
shows Atticus's journey in this book
shows where Atticus has been already
The places Atticus visits in this book
1. Troy
2. Mount Ida
TROY
MOUNT IDA
Lemnos
Iolchus
Mount Pelion
Mt Parnassus
Delphi
Calydon
Ceryneia
Mt Erymanthus
Mt Cyllene
Sikyon
Stymphalus
Corinth
Corydallus
Athens
Euboea
Elis
Mt Cronus
Olympia
Nemea
Mycenae
Tiryns
Argos
Lerna
Aegina
Sparta
Cythera
Seriphos
Delos
Naxos
Chios
Mount Sipylus
Colophon
Mount Latmus
Cydonia
ATTICUS LIVES HERE
Miletus
Mount Ida

Contents

Stories from the Heavens

Long ago, in ancient Greece, gods and goddesses, heroes and heroines lived together with fearful monsters and every kind of

fabulous beast that ever flew, or walked or swam. But little by little, as people began to build more villages and towns and cities, the gods and monsters disappeared into the secret places of the world and the heavens, so that they could have some peace.

Before they disappeared, the gods and goddesses gave the gift of storytelling to men and women, so that nobody would ever forget them. They ordered that there should be a great storytelling festival once every seven years on the slopes of Mount Ida, near Troy, and that tellers of tales should come from all over Greece and from lands near and far to take part.

Every seven years a beautiful painted vase, filled to the brim with gold, magically appeared as a first prize, and the winner was honoured for the rest of his life by all the people of Greece.

It was several days till the competition started, so Atticus hobbled Melissa and left her to graze for the afternoon.

"I'm going down to the shore to get away from the crowds," he said to Callimachus, who reminded him of his son Geryon. "Want to come?"

"Will you tell me a story, then?" asked Callimachus.

"We - ell," Atticus said slowly. "It might stop me feeling so nervous, and they do say practice makes perfect." Callimachus whooped and leaped in the air.

The Hero's Heel

Achilles paced up and down his tent. **Stomp stomp stomp . . . turn . . . stomp, stomp, stomp . . . turn.** His mind was filled with pictures of Polyxena's beautiful face.

"How could she ever love her brother's murderer?" he muttered sadly to himself.

Suddenly, there was a flutter of wings, and a white dove flew through the doorway and landed on his shoulder. It had a message tied to its leg.

read Achilles eagerly.

It was signed with a 'P'.

"'P' for Polyxena," said Achilles. "Maybe she loves me after all."

The day passed as slowly as if it were made of thick dripping treacle. There was no fighting, because the Trojans were still in mourning for their beloved Prince Hector.

Achilles spent the long hours polishing his armour until it would have blinded the sun himself. He sharpened his weapons till they were like razors.

As midnight approached, Achilles put on his best robes over his armour, and strapping a dagger to his side just in case, he sneaked out of the camp and across the plain.

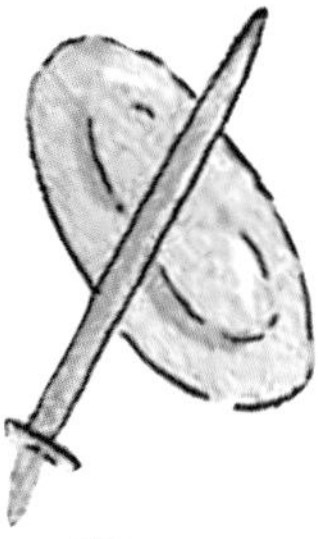

It was a still night, and the moon had not yet risen when he approached the Great Gate. A dark cloaked figure glided out from its shadow.

"Polyxena! My love!" gasped Achilles. But the figure did not speak. It just beckoned.

His heart beating very fast, Achilles followed the figure through a little side door, and through the silent streets of

Troy until it led him into the temple of the god Apollo. Candles were burning around the altar, and the place was heavy with the sweet smells of incense and oil. The figure threw back its hood, and in the dim light, Achilles saw the face of his beloved Polyxena.

"Let us pray to Apollo together," she whispered.

As Achilles knelt down on one knee, his mortal heel was bared.

Hiss! Thunk!

went an arrow, straight into his weak spot.

"Take that, murderer!" cried two voices, and as he looked up in agony, he saw Paris step out from behind a pillar to join his sister Polyxena.

"You!" cried Achilles. "Haven't you caused enough trouble already?"

But Paris just laughed, and Polyxena with him. Wild, high, mad laughter it was, and Achilles had to get away from it.

Stumbling and tripping, he limped back the way he had come, through the winding streets, out of the little door, until he was on the plain again. The pain in his heel was a burning fire now, and he knew that the arrow had been poisoned.

Collapsing in front of the Great Gate of Troy, he remembered Hector's dying words with a shiver.

Then, as he felt the last breath going out of him, he let out a great shriek.

"Mother!" he cried. ***"Mother, save me!"***

And Thetis heard him. Weeping with grief, she came out of the waves followed by her nereid maidens.

But she was too late. As dawn broke she carried her dead son through the sobbing ranks of the Greek army and laid him on a funeral pyre.

For seventeen days and nights the nine Muses chanted a solemn dirge over his ashes, while the Greeks held funeral games in his honour.

"He was the greatest hero of us all," they said. "He will never be forgotten as long as the tale of Troy is told."

And he never has been.

As he finished, Atticus turned to look at Mount Ida to the south.

"So what happened then?" asked Callimachus.

"Well," said Atticus. "The Greeks were in trouble without their hero, Achilles, of course. They'd been in Troy for nearly ten years, and most of them wanted to go home. So Agamemnon asked Calchas the seer to cast an oracle to tell them how it would all turn out in the end."

The Arrows of Death

Calchas staggered out of his tent, plumes of smoke following him from the sacrificial fires. Agamemnon and the other kings watched him, anxious to hear what he had to say about their fates.

"Troy cannot fall, nor Greeks go home,
Till he who's wounded to the bone
With serpent's tooth comes to this shore.
Then Trojan might shall fight no more.
But if he comes, he cannot win
Till hero's son comes riding in.
You need these two, plus arrows and bow
To save you all from strife and woe,"

wheezed Calchas in his cracked old voice.

"But what does it all mean?" asked the kings anxiously. "Who are these men he's talking about?"

Then Odysseus laughed. "One of them is Philoctetes, of course. The one with the smelly wound who owns Heracles' bow and arrows! And the other must be Achilles' son Neoptolemus. Diomedes and I will go and get them."

So off set Odysseus and Diomedes, and while Neoptolemus was delighted to join them, it took every last drop of Odysseus' trickery and cunning to persuade Philoctetes to come to Troy

"Why should I?" said Philoctetes sulkily.

"You all left me here to die. Why should I come and save you now?"

Odysseus took a deep breath. Philoctetes' wound was really very smelly.

"Because Apollo himself has sent a great healer to us, who can cure you (Please, great Apollo, send one! he prayed silently), and when that leg is better the gods themselves say you're going to be the one who punishes the man who began all this (I hope!). Just think how famous you'll be when you kill that traitor, Paris!"

Finally, Odysseus managed to persuade Philoctetes to get into his boat, together with Heracles' bow and arrows.

When they got there, Machaon the famous healer had just arrived. (Thank you, Apollo, thought Odysseus.) In no time at all, Philoctetes was as good as new.

After Hector's death, Paris had been elected leader of the Trojan army, so as soon as he was cured, Philoctetes took his bow and arrows and went to challenge Paris to an archery contest.

"Ho! Traitor!" he called up to the walls. "Come and fight! Or are you going to be a coward and hide behind Helen's skirts?"

Now Paris couldn't bear to be thought a coward, so he took his own bow and arrows and strode out of the gate to face Philoctetes. Both armies stood watching as the two heroes prepared.

Thwack, thwack, thwack! Before Paris could even raise his bow, three of Philoctetes' deadly arrows had hit him. Menelaus ran forward to finish him off, but two Trojan soldiers seized their wounded leader and carried him back to Troy.

"Take me to Mount Ida," groaned Paris, remembering what the nymph Oenone had said when he left her. "My beloved Oenone is the only one who can save me now."

But Oenone did not love Paris any more after the way he had treated her.

"Let that wretched Helen cure him," she sniffed angrily, turning her back. So Paris died in agony, and as his soul fled down to the Underworld, Helen shook her head as if she had suddenly woken up from a dream.

"What am I doing here?" she wailed. "And where is my true husband, Menelaus?"

Aphrodite's love spell had been broken at last, and the war was nearly over.

Next day the steps up to Athene's Temple were crowded with people. Atticus asked Callimachus to hold Melissa while he went up to make his sacrifice.

"For the Goddess," he whispered, handing his jar of wine to a priestess.

"May she give you a tongue of silk, and the voice of a nightingale!" boomed the priestess. Everybody looked at Atticus and pointed.

"How on earth did that woman know I was in the competition?" he asked Callimachus. Callimachus pointed to the carved red entry stick poking out of Atticus's pocket.

"Easy!" he said. "Now how about another story?"

The Luck of Troy

Now that Paris was dead, the kings met once more to discuss how they were to defeat Troy and rescue Helen.

"We have done everything that Calchas advised," they said. "So why hasn't Troy surrendered?"

Just then Odysseus came in with a prisoner. It was the Trojan prophet Helenus, who had been captured on his way from Troy to Mount Ida.

"Tell us how we can defeat your city, old man!" cried the kings.

But Helenus would not betray his people. "All I will say is this," he said.

"A magic statue protects us from harm, and while we have it, Troy will never fall!" Then he went on his way.

"It's up to you, Odysseus," said the kings. "You must sneak into Troy somehow and find out where this magic statue is kept. Then you must steal it and bring it back to us."

It was the most difficult thing Odysseus had ever had to do. How was he to get into the city without being found out? Finally, he dressed up as a beggar and got Diomedes to beat him until the blood ran. Then he crawled to the gate of the city.

"Help me! Help me!" he begged. "Save me from the dreadful Greeks, especially that terrible Odysseus who has given me these painful wounds."

The Trojan soldiers took him to King Priam at once. The kind old man had his wounds bathed, and gave him a fresh cloak and a hot meal, and after asking him some questions, to which Odysseus replied with clever lies, he set him free.

"You may live with us," said Priam. "We need all the soldiers we can get."

Now Helen had recognised Odysseus at once, and as he left Priam's palace, she ran after him and beckoned him up to her bedroom.

"You've got to save me and take me back to my dear Menelaus," she said.

"I must have been under a spell to run off with that spoilt boy Paris!" Then Odysseus asked her where he could find the magic statue.

"It is called the Luck of Troy, and it's in the Temple of Pallas Athene," she said. "If you stay here with me, I will take you there at nightfall."

They spent a delightful afternoon together plotting and planning the defeat of Troy, then, as it grew dark, they went out to the temple.

While Helen distracted the old priestess, Odysseus tiptoed behind the

temple pillars and seized the statue from the chest behind the altar. Helen had shown him a secret passage under the walls, and soon he had escaped, muddy but triumphant.

"We have the Luck of Troy, Your Majesties," he said, as he strolled into the Greek camp, holding up the precious object. "I think we can defeat them now! Helen and I have worked out a brilliant plan."

The Trojans shivered in their beds as they heard the wild cheers break out from the ships by the shore. But Helen only smiled.

"I shall soon be free!" she whispered eagerly. "Watch out Troy, the Greeks are coming!"

A day later, they were standing together on the slope by the Great Gate of Troy.

"This is where the Wooden Horse stood, isn't it?" asked Callimachus.

"Yes," said Atticus. "My old grandfather used to say it was taller than twenty men."

Callimachus's eyes were round with wonder. "Please, Atticus. Please tell me the story. I'll do anything for you . . ."

Atticus laughed. It looked as if Callimachus of Cyrene was bringing him luck already!

The Wooden Horse

The ramparts of Troy were crowded as everybody tried to see what the Greeks were doing behind their high wall. Such a hammering and banging, such a bustle and hustle hadn't been heard or seen since they had arrived, ten whole years ago.

"They'll attack tomorrow," said the gloomy ones among them, as they heard the sound of axes being sharpened.

But as the next day dawned, bright and sunny, the Trojans had a great surprise when they looked out from the ramparts again. No tents, no horses, no men, no ships, no fires – not a trace of the Greeks was left on the shore. Only

the high wall remained, and behind that was something so strange that the Trojans poured out of the gates to look at it.

It was a huge wooden horse, the height of twenty men. Its mane was painted royal purple, it had great staring eyes made of red and green stones, and its harness was painted gold on its jet-black body.

There was a notice tied around its neck.

AN OFFERING TO ATHENE FOR OUR SAFE RETURN TO GREECE

it said in large letters.

The Trojans danced and sang with joy. They were free at last!

"Let us take this beautiful thing into the city, and put it in front of Athene's temple!" they cried. But Priam and his counsellors were not so sure.

"Perhaps it is a trick," they said. "Perhaps an army of heroes is hiding inside!" So they stuck spears into the horse's belly, and wiggled them around. But not a sound was heard.

Then Helen stepped forward.

"I have an idea," she said. "If there are Greek heroes hiding in there, they will not be able to resist the sound of their wives' voices – after all they haven't seen them for

ten years. When I was born, the gods gave me the gift of imitation. I can imitate all their wives so perfectly that if the heroes are in there, they will come out straight away."

Priam and his counsellors thought this was brilliant, so Helen walked round the horse calling each hero by name.

"Oh Odysseus," she called in Penelope's voice. "Oh Menelaus, beloved, it is I, your Helen."

Each of the heroes she called in turn, but none replied, as she had arranged with Odysseus.

"There," she said to Priam. "You see, it's perfectly safe."

So the Trojans pulled the horse into the city. It was so huge that they had to take the gates off their hinges to get it through, but at last it was pulled to its resting-place in front of Athene's temple.

Everybody was so exhausted that they went to bed very early.

"We will dedicate the horse to Athene in the morning," they murmured sleepily.

But in the dead of night a trapdoor in the horse's belly opened, and out poured all the heroes of the Greek army.

Helen flashed a bright light from her window to call back the Greek ships which had been hiding behind some islands, and soon they were on their way to Troy once more.

Then the heroes cut down the sleepy sentries guarding the open gates and the palace – all except for Menelaus who ran to find Helen.

The defeat of Troy had begun.

It was the day before the competition started, and everybody was making their way to the amphitheatre on Mount Ida to make sure of a good spot. Several people were clutching carved coloured sticks like Atticus's red one.

"I was wondering . . ." said Callimachus from Melissa's other side.

"Whether I could tell you a story," finished Atticus. "I'm not sure I should. It might look like showing off with all these other storytellers around."

"Oh, go on," said Callimachus. "No one will hear you except me. And you did promise to tell me about the sack of Troy . . ."

The Greeks Go Home

Many dreadful deeds were done in the streets of Troy that night, and few escaped. The Greeks showed little mercy, and soon the sky was lit with flames and smoke, and the cries of the wounded were heard even by the gods on Olympus. Hera and Athene looked at each other and smiled. Their revenge on Paris's birthplace was nearly complete.

Menelaus fought his way through the streets, killing anyone who got in his way. He was desperate to reach his wife. At last he found the house where Odysseus had told him she lived and ran up the stairs. At the door stood one of Hector's brothers,

Deiophobus, with his sword drawn.

"You shall not have her," he snarled. But Zeus himself gave strength to Menelaus's arm, and soon Deiophobus lay dead. Menelaus stepped over his body, and went into the room. There was Helen, sitting on the bed, weeping.

He looked at her and remembered all the sorrow she had caused for both Greeks and Trojans alike. But she was still as beautiful as ever, and as she looked up, the tears running down her lovely cheeks like crystal drops of dew, his heart melted, and he dropped his bloody sword and held out his arms.

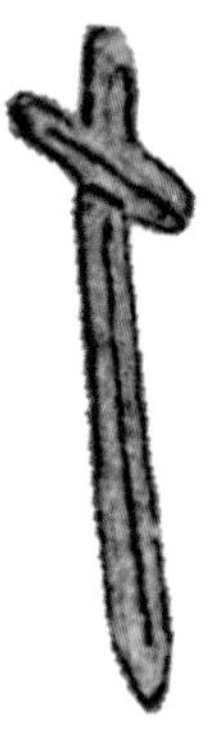

"It was not your fault, my love," he said quietly. "It was the will of the gods. Will you come home to Greece with me?" And Helen ran to him and kissed him and kissed him as if she would never stop.

As they walked away together towards the Greek ships, hand in hand, the city of Troy went up in fountains of fire. The spires of the palace came crashing down, and the tall gate towers crumbled into a heap of stone.

As dawn broke, only a smoking ruin was left. The great city of Troy was no more and the long war was over at last.

"And then did they all just go home?" asked Callimachus as they arrived on the lower slopes of the mountain. Atticus looked round. He could hear the crash of thunder in the distance.

"Looks like a sea-storm's building," he said. "Let's make ourselves and Melissa a proper shelter under this boulder, and then I'll tell you the last story about the Trojan War. After that I shall have to rest my voice. It's my big day tomorrow, and you wouldn't want me to be hoarse!"

The Princess Nobody Believed

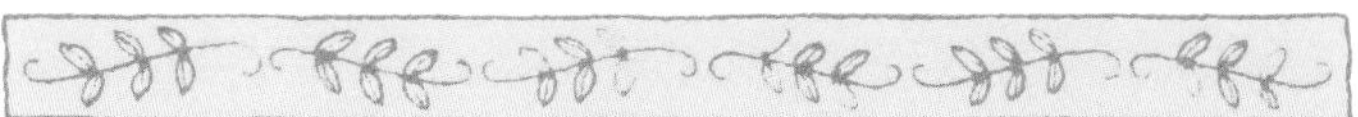

The Greeks were now free to return to their homes and families after ten long years. They loaded their ships with looted treasures and slaves, and prepared to depart. But as the sails went up, a fierce wind rose, preventing them from leaving the harbour.

"Not again!" groaned Menelaus and Agamemnon, and they sent for Calchas the soothsayer to find out what the problem was.

Now one of the Greek heroes was a man called Ajax. He was a strong, brave man, and a brilliant runner and javelin player. But he also had a terrible temper.

When the belly of the wooden horse had opened, he had been one of the first out. He had headed straight for the Temple of Athene, where he knew there would be plenty of treasure.

"And perhaps I shall capture some slaves, too," he thought greedily.

Ajax liked owning slaves. It made him feel important. As he entered the temple, he noticed a girl hiding behind a pillar.

His first slave! He dragged her out by the hair and tied her up, even though she screamed and clung to the altar and prayed out loud to the goddess.

"Woe!" screamed the girl. "Woe to him who makes the priestess Cassandra a slave. He shall be struck by Zeus himself!"

But Ajax took no notice, and anyway he didn't believe that the ruler of the universe was going to bother about one puny slave girl, even if she did claim to be some priestess.

How wrong he was!

Little did Ajax know that Cassandra was the daughter of King Priam.

One day she had been picking violets by a stream when Apollo had come by. He had fallen in love with the beautiful princess. But she would have nothing to do with him.

"I am going to be a seer and tell the future," she said. "I don't have time to fall in love with gods."

This made Apollo so furious that he put a terrible curse on her.

"You will indeed see the future, Cassandra – in fact you will be my sister Athene's priestess," he said. "But the trouble is that nobody will believe what you say."

And it was true – Cassandra predicted all sorts of things, some good, some bad

– but no one ever believed a word of it.

Calchas closed his eyes and looked for a sign from the gods. Quite soon he began to speak. He told Menelaus and the other kings how badly Ajax had treated Cassandra.

"He must be punished," he cried loudly. "For the gods themselves have marked her for their own." Ajax was furious. He lost his temper completely and tried to fight everyone who came aboard his ship. But finally Cassandra was saved and taken back to the shore.

"I don't believe in the wretched gods!" cried Ajax, shaking his fist at the sky. The wind dropped for a moment, and he ordered his ship to set sail at once. "I don't need any of you," he yelled in a rage.

It does not do to mock the gods, and as soon as Ajax's ship had left the safety

of the harbour, it hit a huge rock. The ship began to sink.

"Come and get me, Zeus!" cried Ajax, laughing madly and dancing on the tilting deck. This was too much. Zeus sent down a thunderbolt while Poseidon aimed his trident and together they sank Ajax and his ship to the bottom of the sea.

Then the winds fell and the waves were calm, and the rest of the Greek fleet sailed away from Troy for ever. But not all of them reached home, and some travelled a long and weary road, and had many adventures before they got there.

Troy was rebuilt in time, but it was never again as great as it had been under King Priam and his brave sons and daughters.

Early on the first day of the competition, a single trumpet note rang out to call everyone to the amphitheatre.

Atticus hurried towards the arena, straightening his best robes and clutching his red stick and the lucky pebble his children had given him before he left Crete. Two hundred and forty-nine other storytellers hurried with him. When the sacrifices to the gods were over, the Thirty-Ninth Mount Ida storytelling festival was declared open.

"We will now draw the stories for each group of competitors," shouted the chief judge. He stuck his hand into a big leather bag and pulled out a red stick. Then he stuck his other hand into a huge brass jar and pulled out a slip of parchment.

"Red Group!" he cried. Atticus and twenty-four others moved forward nervously. "You will each tell a story about Odysseus." The crowd cheered.

Minutes later the Red Group judges had given everyone a numbered disc.

Atticus looked down at his. "One" it said in large letters. He was first. Slowly he walked out in front of the judges and began.

The Land of Sleep

Of all the heroes who conquered Troy, Odysseus, King of Ithaca was the most cunning. He was craftier than a fox, cleverer than a snake, and wilier than a wolf in goat's clothing. But even he could not escape the fate that Zeus had planned for him, although he tried very hard.

"Perhaps Zeus has forgotten that he told the oracle I couldn't go home for another ten years," he said to himself. "Maybe if I just sail home very quietly, Zeus won't notice." So he sneaked away from Troy with his twelve ships and set a course for Ithaca.

Almost immediately a great storm blew up, and the ships were blown hither and thither, up and down and round and round, until their sails were in rags and their sailors were drooping with weariness.

"Oh dear!" said Odysseus on the ninth day, when the winds had died down and the ships had come to rest on a strange shore far far away from his beloved home. "Zeus hasn't forgotten me after all." But he was a brave man, and he wasn't going to be put off by a little bad luck.

"This looks like an interesting place," he said to his sailors, and he sent out three of his men to go and explore, while he and the others mended the ships as best they could, or rested in the warm sunshine.

Hours went by, and more hours, and soon it was getting dark. The men had not returned.

"I suppose I shall have to go out and look for them," sighed Odysseus.

Now the place where Odysseus and his ships had landed was filled with a strange forgetting magic. The people who lived there were called the Lotus-Eaters. They were all very beautiful and they ate nothing but a sweet juice which they made from the petals of a white flower that grew in the pools and rivers.

They dressed in robes of gold and silver, and they lived high in the treetops, where they sang like birds, and danced in the branches.

Odysseus tramped through the dark forest all night, but just after sunrise he came to a green glade, with a silver cloth spread in the middle of it. His three men were sprawled asleep on the grass, each clutching a golden cup.

Above him sounded faint laughter and the twittering of birdsong. He shook the men roughly and their sleepy eyes opened.

"Noo!" they groaned. "Go away, who-ever you are! We want more lotus juice!"

"Come on, you three," said Odysseus sternly. "What about your wives and children waiting at home in Ithaca?" But the men just smiled stupidly and asked him where Ithaca was.

"More lotus juice," they cried. "More wonderful, marvellous lotus juice is all we want for the rest of our lives."
The treetops shook and shivered with invisible giggles as the Lotus-Eaters looked down on Odysseus and his men.

In the end poor Odysseus had to go back all the long, long way through the forest and fetch the rest of the crew to drag them back to the ships.

And for days afterwards the three men had to be tied to the mast to stop them jumping into the sea and trying to swim back to the land of the Lotus-Eaters.

"Let's try again," said Odysseus as he gave the order to set sail for Ithaca once more. But Odysseus's adventures weren't over yet – oh no! Zeus had planned many many more exciting things for the years to come, and his return to Ithaca was a long, long way off.

The judge was reading out the list of those who had got through to the second day. Atticus hugged Callimachus when he heard his name called.

"I did it!" he cried.

"Of course you did," snorted Callimachus. "You were the best by far. Now hush! You're supposed to listen."

The judge was talking again. "Those in the two Copper Groups will each tell five stories. One today, and two on each of the following days."

When he had finished explaining, he handed each competitor a copper disc.

"What did you get?" asked Callimachus.

"The story about the Cyclops," Atticus whispered. "One of my favourites."

The One-Eyed Giant

On the island of Sicily there lived a most terrible giant called Polyphemus, together with his six brothers. He was a son of Poseidon, and he was one of the race of Cyclopes, who only have one huge bright blue eye, set right in the middle of their foreheads.

Now after Odysseus had left the land of the Lotus-Eaters, Zeus had sent another great storm, which had blown him and his ships this way and that and back and forth until they didn't know where they were or what day of the week it was. So when they saw a huge grassy island, covered in the most wonderful fat sheep and goats, they were overjoyed.

"Drop the anchors!" cried Odysseus. "Lower the boats! We will take a few jars of our best wine and buy some of those sheep from whoever owns them. Then we will all have a big feast."

The sailors danced and cheered, because they were all very hungry after so long at sea.

Odysseus and eleven of his best men got into the boats and rowed for the shore. When they had landed, they walked up a steep rocky path, carrying the wine carefully so as not to drop it, until they came to an enormous cave.

"Pick out some nice juicy-looking sheep while we're waiting for the shepherd to come home," ordered Odysseus. "We don't want to waste any time."

Just as the men had driven ten fat sheep into the cave, they heard a roaring and a stamping and the rocks around them began to shake. Terrified, they ran to the back of the cave and hid behind a large stone. In marched a dreadful looking giant. He sat down in the doorway and called out in a harsh voice:

"Come, come my flocks and herds. Come to Polyphemus and be milked."

Odysseus gasped. He had heard of Polyphemus and he knew they were in trouble. When Polyphemus had finished, he lit a crackling fire in the cave. As the flames grew bright, he noticed the twelve Ithacans hiding behind the stone.

He gave a great roar of anger. **"Strangers!"** he growled. **"Sheep-stealers!** I shall tear you limb from limb, and eat you for my supper!"

And the next second he had seized two of Odysseus's men and had stuffed them into his mouth and crunched them up.

Then he rolled a heavy boulder in front of the cave entrance and lay down to sleep.

As his snores echoed round the cave, Odysseus tried frantically to think of a plan. But it was no good.

The next morning the giant seized two more of his men and crunched them up as before. Then he went out to see to his flocks, rolling the boulder back behind him as he went. Odysseus and his men were trapped!

As he paced up and down in the dim light, trying to think, Odysseus noticed a large log of wood lying on the ground. It gave him an idea.

"Come on, you men," he called. "Come and help me sharpen this to a point."

"We shall all be eaten up!" groaned his men despairingly. But Odysseus chivvied them and bullied them until he had a long sharp pointed stake.

Just as he was hiding it in a corner, Polyphemus came back. As before, he milked his flocks, and then he grabbed two more men and ate them.

He burped loudly and lay back after rolling the boulder in front of the door, but this time he didn't go to sleep. At once Odysseus stepped forward.

"Perhaps you would like some wine after your meal, great Cyclops!" he said timidly. The giant reached out his enormous hand.

"Don't mind if I do," he said. "Tell me your name, little shrimp, so that I can drink your health."

"My name is Nobody," said Odysseus cunningly.

"Very well, Nobody," said the giant. "If you give me some more of this wine I shall give you a gift. I shall promise to eat you last of all your men!"

And he laughed horribly, and glugged down another jar. Soon he was snoring like a volcano.

"Right, men," said Odysseus. "Let's get out of here." They heated the point of the stake in the fire and then with a great heave they plunged it into Polyphemus's eye and blinded him.

The giant leaped up with a roar and danced around the cave. Sheep, goats and men scattered out of the way of his galumphing feet.

He made so much noise that his six brothers came to see what was happening.

"Who is hurting you?" they cried.

"Nobody!" yelled Polyphemus. "Nobody is!" The other giants looked at each other and shrugged.

"He must have a bad belly-ache," they said to each other as they went away.

Early the next morning as Polyphemus rolled the boulder away to let out his flocks, Odysseus tied his five remaining men underneath the five largest sheep.

Odysseus himself clung underneath the ram, holding his breath as Polyphemus felt along each sheep's back to see if he and his men were escaping. As soon as

they were out of the cave they ran back to the boats as fast as they could, taking as many sheep as would fit.

How relieved they all were to sail away from that terrible island. But as they sailed past Polyphemus's cave, Odysseus made a big mistake.

"Ho! Polyphemus!" he shouted. "You have not been tricked by Nobody after all. I am King Odysseus of Ithaca!"

Polyphemus heard him, and roared out a curse.

"Let my father, Poseidon, god of the sea, punish you!" he cried. And Poseidon heard him. Now Odysseus had not one, but two powerful gods working against him. Would he ever get home to Ithaca after this?

Greek Beasts and Heroes and where to find them …

Imagine living all alone on an island with only a horrid 'smelly wound' for company. But how did Philoctetes end up like that? Read about it if you dare in *The Hero's Spear*.

There are lots of dangerous archers in Atticus's stories – not just Philoctetes in "The Arrows of Death". Heracles took a bow and arrow with him when he was ordered to steal Geryon's cows – but did he succeed? Find out in

"Cattle Stealer" (in *The Fire Breather,* which contains several stories about Heracles' amazing labours). Or maybe you'd like to read about Atalanta the Brave Huntress, who carried a bigger bow than many heroes twice her size. She's in *The Harp of Death.*

Ajax was famous for his terrible temper. To find out whose anger caused a ferocious storm to come from nowhere, look for

"The Dolphin's Message" in the book with the same title. What happened when Pan lost his temper with the beautiful Reed Nymph called Syrinx? You'll have to read *The Silver Chariot* to find out the answer.

Atticus knows lots more stories about princesses – like the beautiful one King Aegeus secretly married. He had to leave her behind – but he never forgot her. What

happened to their son is told in the story of "The Robber's Bed" in *The Dolphin's Message*. Or you might like the princess shut up by her cruel father in "The Copper Tower". Did she ever escape? Find out in *The Magic Head*.

Odysseus was the most cunning of heroes – and his grandfather Autolycus was pretty clever too. Read all about "The Cunning Thief" in *The Flying Horse*.

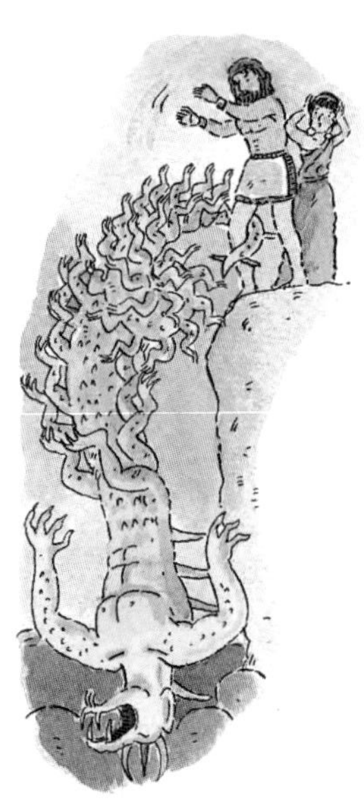

Are giants your favourite monsters? How about finding more of them in the tale of "The War of the Snake Giants"? Look out for *The Harp of Death* again.